TRON
LEGACY

INTO THE LIGHT

Written by Tennant Redbank
Based on the screenplay written by Eddy Kitsis & Adam Horowitz
Based on characters created by Steven Lisberger and Bonnie MacBird
Executive Producer Donald Kushner
Produced by Sean Bailey, Jeffrey Silver, Steven Lisberger
Directed by Joseph Kosinski

DISNEP PRESS
NEW YORK

Copyright © 2010 Disney Enterprises, Inc. All rights reserved. Published by Disney Press, an imprint of Disney Book Group. No part of this book may be reproduced or transmitted in any form or by any means, electronic or mechanical, including photocopying, recording, or by any information storage and retrieval system, without written permission from the publisher. For information address Disney Press, 114 Fifth Avenue, New York, New York 10011-5690.

Printed in the United States of America

First Edition
1 3 5 7 9 10 8 6 4 2
G658-7729-4-10244

Library of Congress Catalog Card Number on file.
ISBN 978-1-4231-3151-9

Visit Disneybooks.com

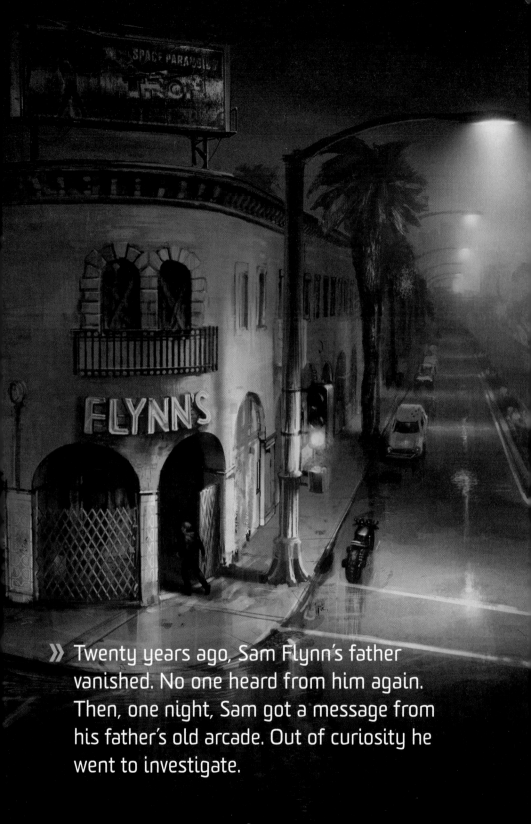

» Twenty years ago, Sam Flynn's father vanished. No one heard from him again. Then, one night, Sam got a message from his father's old arcade. Out of curiosity he went to investigate.

» Inside, the old machines were covered in dust and cobwebs. When Sam went to play his favorite game, Tron, he found a secret door. It led to his father's lab!

Sam took a seat at a desk. A light flashed. Then nothing. Sam left. There were no answers there.

» Outside, the air was thick with fog. Rain fell. The street in front of the arcade looked different to Sam. Something had changed.

Suddenly, a spotlight lit up the dark. Sam squinted up at it. Was it a helicopter?

No! It was a Recognizer!

Sam's dad had given him a toy just like it when he was younger.

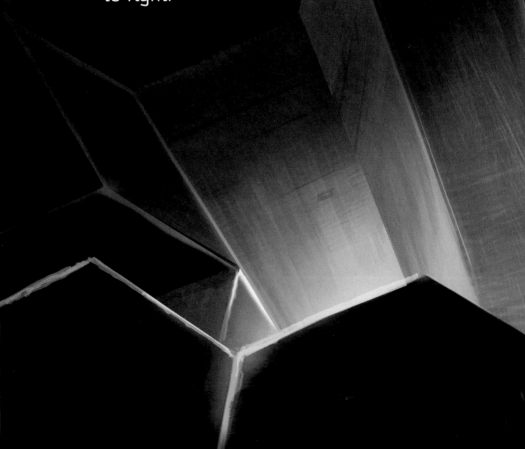

» Somehow he had gotten zapped into the digital world known as the Grid.

Sam started to run.

"*Identify yourself, program!*" boomed a robotlike voice.

"Wait!" Sam yelled. But it was too late. The Recognizer pulled him off the street. He was now a captive.

And in this world, captives were forced to fight.

» Four beautiful programs called Sirens gave Sam armor to wear. Then he was given a disc. The disc held everything that made him who he was. Finally Sam was dropped into the gladiatorial arena.

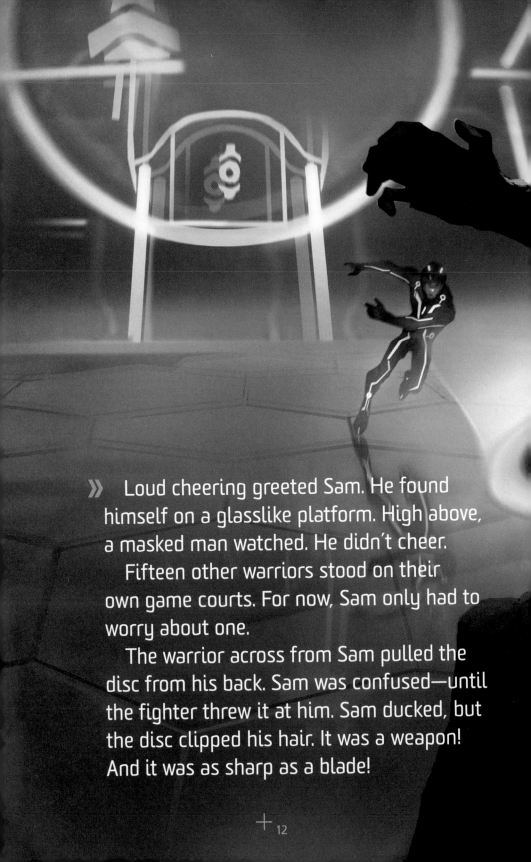

» Loud cheering greeted Sam. He found himself on a glasslike platform. High above, a masked man watched. He didn't cheer.

Fifteen other warriors stood on their own game courts. For now, Sam only had to worry about one.

The warrior across from Sam pulled the disc from his back. Sam was confused—until the fighter threw it at him. Sam ducked, but the disc clipped his hair. It was a weapon! And it was as sharp as a blade!

》 "All right, here we go," Sam said. He pulled his own disc free and fired it at the warrior. The disc missed and came back.

Meanwhile, the other warrior leaped to Sam's glass platform. He raised his disc like an ax. Sam rolled away. With his disc, Sam broke the glass under the program's feet. The program dropped into the void.

Right away, a new warrior faced Sam.

"Hey! Can I get a time-out?" Sam yelled.

No one answered.

» The game went on. Sam did very well. In the ship that hovered above the arena, the masked man took notice of this new warrior.

Soon Sam had made it to the final contest. He was battling the top warrior, Rinzler. Rinzler fought with two discs! He whipped them at Sam. Sam could not dodge both. One sliced his arm. He was hurt. Rinzler paused. He and the other warriors were not human. They were computer programs. They did not bleed.

» Rinzler was not the only one to notice.
"Identify yourself," a voice ordered
from above.

"My name is Sam Flynn!" Sam shouted.

The crowd gasped. They knew the name
Flynn. There were legends about Kevin
Flynn, the man who had made the Grid.
Some programs even thought he was still
living in their world.

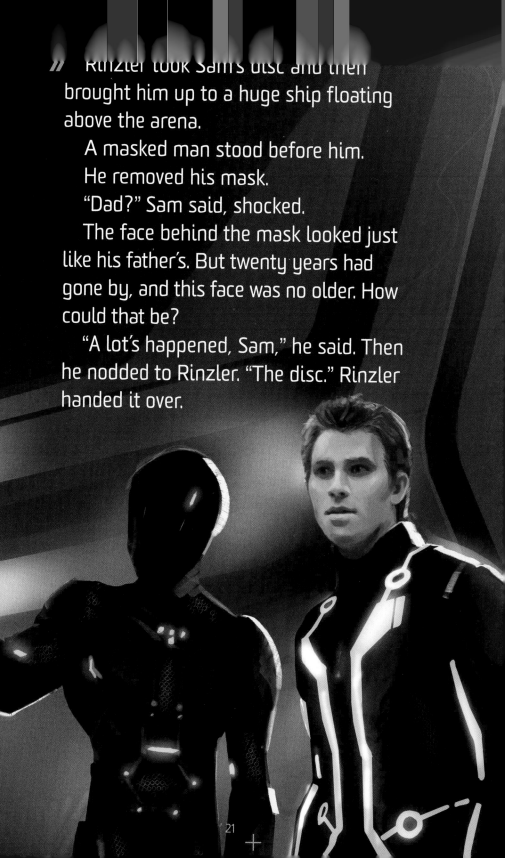

Rinzler took Sam's disc and then brought him up to a huge ship floating above the arena.

A masked man stood before him.

He removed his mask.

"Dad?" Sam said, shocked.

The face behind the mask looked just like his father's. But twenty years had gone by, and this face was no older. How could that be?

"A lot's happened, Sam," he said. Then he nodded to Rinzler. "The disc." Rinzler handed it over.

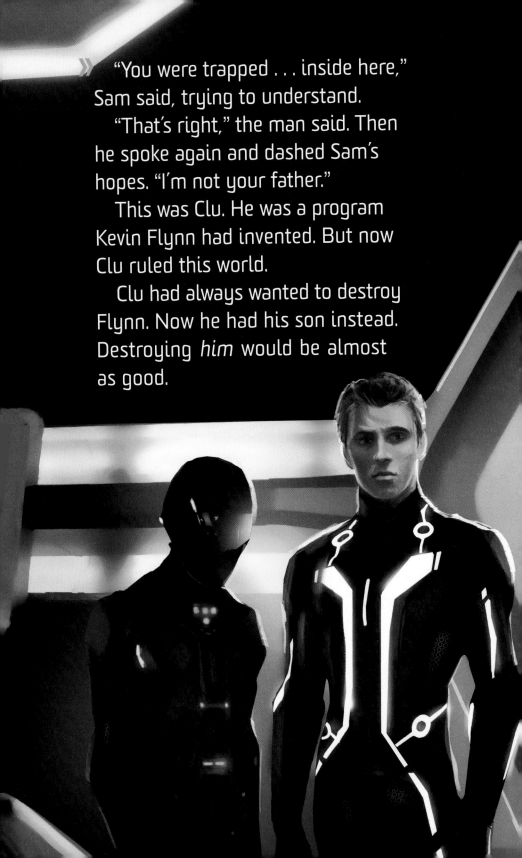

"You were trapped . . . inside here," Sam said, trying to understand.

"That's right," the man said. Then he spoke again and dashed Sam's hopes. "I'm not your father."

This was Clu. He was a program Kevin Flynn had invented. But now Clu ruled this world.

Clu had always wanted to destroy Flynn. Now he had his son instead. Destroying *him* would be almost as good.

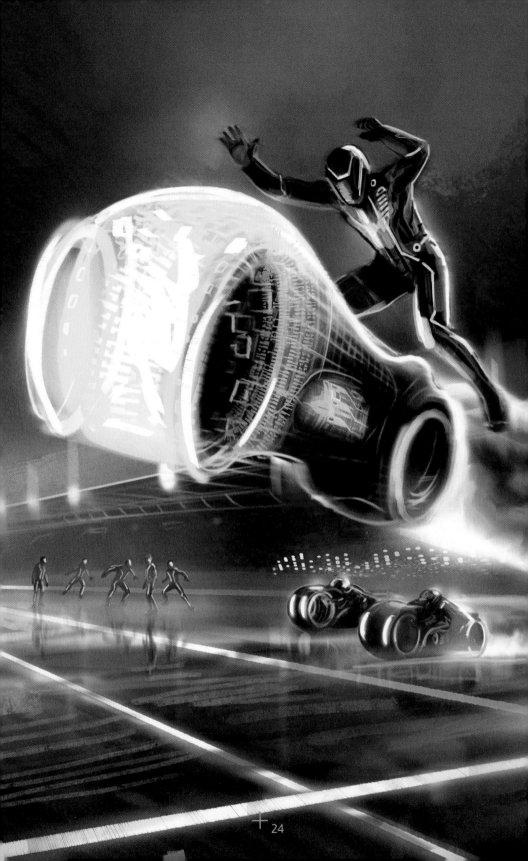

The throne ship dropped down onto what looked like a racetrack. Clu took off his cape.

"You want to play?" Sam said to Clu. The man nodded.

They each took a rod from a nearby chest. Clu's was yellow. Sam's was white. "What do I do with this?" Sam asked.

Clu gripped the rod in both hands. He sprinted forward and leaped into the air. The rod became a Light Cycle!

Sam's eyes grew wide. He could do that. In an instant, his white rod became a Light Cycle, too.

»   The cycles zoomed out. Behind each bike, a wall of colored lights formed. The wall was deadly. Crash into it and it was game over.

    Sam and Clu raced side by side. *Whack!* Clu rammed into Sam. Sam tumbled off his bike.

    Clu bore down on him. He pulled out his disc. He moved in for the kill.

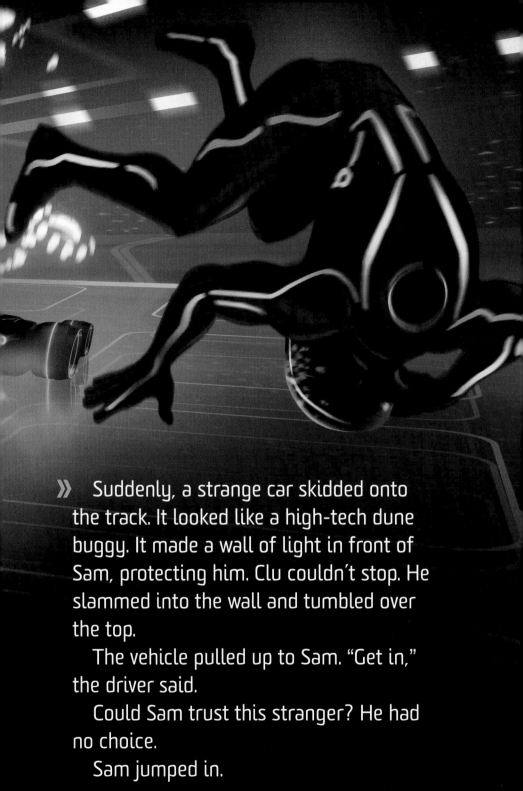

>> Suddenly, a strange car skidded onto the track. It looked like a high-tech dune buggy. It made a wall of light in front of Sam, protecting him. Clu couldn't stop. He slammed into the wall and tumbled over the top.

The vehicle pulled up to Sam. "Get in," the driver said.

Could Sam trust this stranger? He had no choice.

Sam jumped in.

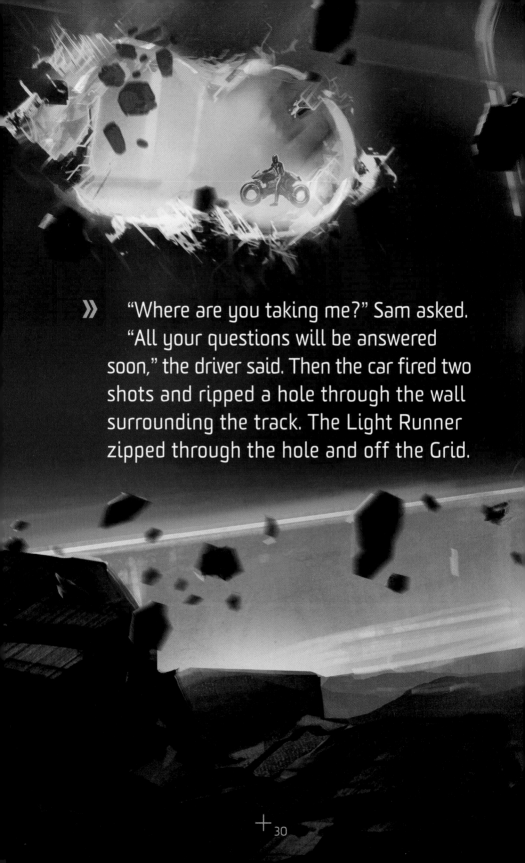

» "Where are you taking me?" Sam asked. "All your questions will be answered soon," the driver said. Then the car fired two shots and ripped a hole through the wall surrounding the track. The Light Runner zipped through the hole and off the Grid.

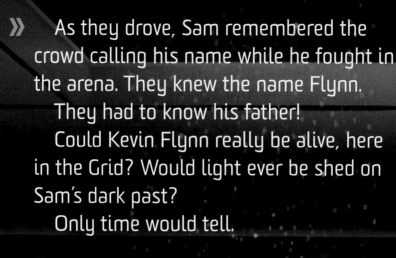

» As they drove, Sam remembered the crowd calling his name while he fought in the arena. They knew the name Flynn.

They had to know his father!

Could Kevin Flynn really be alive, here in the Grid? Would light ever be shed on Sam's dark past?

Only time would tell.